Cassandra Who?

Cassandra Who?

By Iris Hiskey · Illustrated by Normand Chartier

SIMON & SCHUSTER BOOKS FOR YOUNG READERS

Published by Simon & Schuster

New York · London · Toronto · Sydney · Tokyo · Singapore

SIMON & SCHUSTER BOOKS FOR YOUNG READERS
Simon & Schuster Building
Rockefeller Center
1230 Avenue of the Americas
New York, New York 10020

SIMON & SCHUSTER BOOKS FOR YOUNG READERS
is a trademark of Simon & Schuster.

Designed by Vicki Kalajian

The text of this book is set in 14 pt. Paragon.
The illustrations were done in watercolor.

Manufactured in Hong Kong

10 9 8 7 6 5 4 3 2 1

Library of Congress Cataloging-in-Publication Data
Hiskey, Iris. Cassandra who? / written by Iris Hiskey ;
illustrated by Normand Chartier.   Summary: When Cassandra
the cat is invited to a costume party by someone
she doesn't even know, the confusion begins.
I. Chartier, Normand, 1945-   ill.   II. Title.   PZ7.A7343Cas
1991   [E]—dc20   90-37564   ISBN: 0-671-70574-1
[1. Cats—Fiction. 2. Animals—Fiction. 3. Parties—Fiction. 4. Costume—Fiction.]

To my father, Clarence F. Hiskey,
who has dedicated so much of
his life to me

I.H.

Matthew,
will you please come to my party?

N.C.

One Friday morning, when Cassandra stepped out onto her porch to water the flowers, she saw the mail carrier coming down the road.

"Anything for me today, Maisie?" she called.

The mail carrier looked up.

"Sorry," he said, "I'm Marvin. Maisie's on vacation this week. If you'll tell me who you are, I'll see if I have anything for you."

"I'm Cassandra," she said, "and I hope I get something really exciting in the mail today."

The mail carrier looked through his pouch.

"Cassandra, Cassandra...yup, here's something," he said, and handed her a big yellow envelope decorated with hearts and stars and planets.

You are invited to a COSTUME PARTY tomorrow afternoon at Two O'clock at my house – 13 Turtle Cove Road. PRIZES for the best costumes,

Amy

"Thanks," she said. "This does look pretty exciting." Inside the envelope was a bright green card shaped like a turtle. It read:

"A costume party!" cried Cassandra. "My favorite kind! But who is Amy, and why did she invite me?" Cassandra was puzzled.

"One of my friends must know her," she thought.

"That must be it. That's how I got invited."

Cassandra had a wonderful idea for a costume. She spent all day making it.

On Saturday, right after lunch, Cassandra put on the costume. When she looked in the mirror, she was so pleased she danced a little jig.

"This is my best costume ever," she said proudly and blew a kiss to herself. From the mirror, a little pink pig with a blue bow on its tail blew a kiss back.

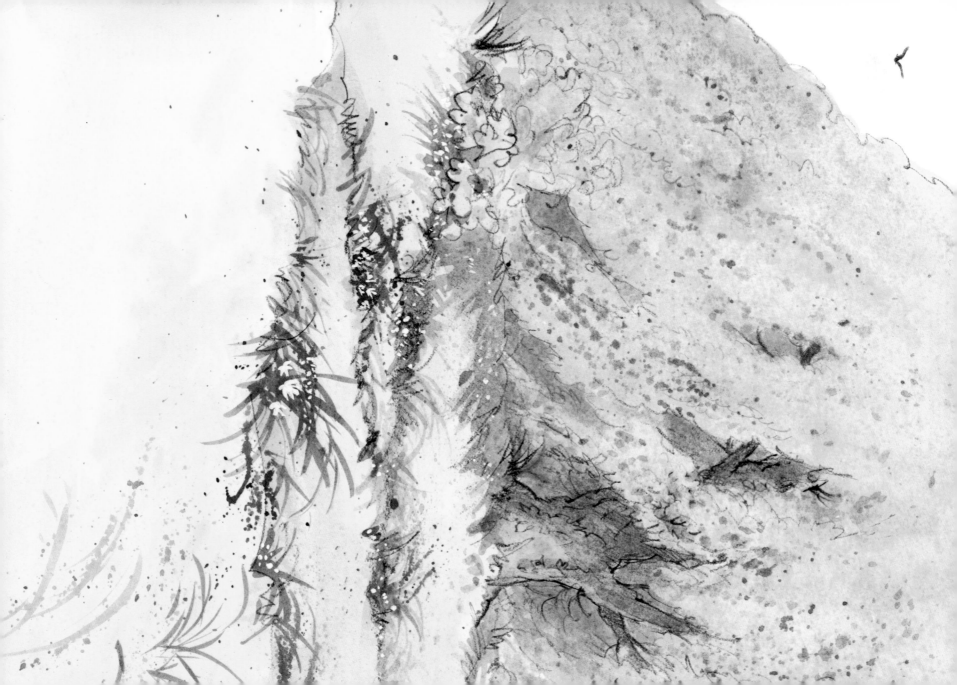

"I'm sure that no one will recognize me," thought Cassandra as she skipped down the path toward Turtle Cove Road. The sun was shining brightly, the breezes blew softly, and Cassandra felt as happy as any fluffy cat disguised as a little pink pig with a blue bow on her tail possibly could.

After a while, she came to Turtle Cove Road and followed the numbers to Amy's house. She danced up the steps and knocked on the door. Inside she could hear laughing and singing.

The door was opened by a sheep in an angel costume.

"Hi, Cassandra," said the sheep. "Come on in. Everyone's here, and we've been waiting for you!" She turned and went back into the house.

"But wait!" Cassandra cried. "Who are you, and how do you know my name?" The party was very noisy and the sheep didn't hear her.

Cassandra walked in. She saw a goat dressed like a gypsy and a dog in a space suit. The goat was playing a piano and the dog was singing. There was a cow dressed like a barn and a chicken dressed like a witch. They were dancing together. Cassandra didn't know anyone.

"Cassandra," mooed the cow, looking straight at her.
"Where's your costume?"

"I'm...I'm wearing it," stammered Cassandra.

"Maybe she just didn't feel like dressing up," said the dog.

"But I did dress up!" said Cassandra. She felt as if she was about to cry.

"Don't mind them, Cassandra," said the chicken.

"I love your blue bow."

"Maybe she didn't have time to make a costume," said the goat.

"This is all very strange," thought Cassandra.

"Cassandra's my best friend, and she can wear any costume she likes to my party," said the sheep.

"I'm Amy's best friend?" wondered Cassandra.

"This must be a dream."

"Come on, everybody," said Amy. "It's time to hand out prizes."

All the guests formed a circle around her.

Amy cleared her throat loudly.

"The prize for Most Heavenly Costume," she said, "goes, of course, to me!"

Everyone clapped as she pinned a big gold star on the front of her angel costume.

"The prize for Biggest Costume," continued Amy, "goes to Lester." The cow in the barn costume proudly accepted a purple star.

Cassandra watched as the goat dressed like a gypsy got a rainbow-colored star for Most Colorful Costume, the dog in the space suit got a green star for Most Out-of-This-World Costume, and the chicken dressed like a witch got an orange star for Scariest Costume.

"And now for Cassandra," said Amy. "Let me see...." Suddenly there was a loud pounding, and a small pink pig wearing a sparkling crown and a long purple cape burst angrily through the door.

"Why didn't you invite me to your party, Amy?" she cried. "I thought you were my best friend, but I heard about the party from two squirrels talking outside my window!"

"Of course I invited you," said Amy, "and you...you came an hour ago!"

"What?" cried the pig.

"But...look!" said Amy, pointing at Cassandra. "That's ridiculous! I just got here!"

"Who are *you?*" cried the pig.
"I'm Cassandra," she said.
"No you're not!" cried the pig. "*I am!*"

"I'm Cassandra the cat," she said, pulling off the top of her costume, "and now I'm beginning to understand."

Everyone gasped when they saw Cassandra's fluffy head and long whiskers sticking out of the pig costume.

"But how did you know about the party?" asked Amy.

"You sent me an invitation," said Cassandra, holding out the yellow envelope.

"I didn't know there were two Cassandras when I put the invitation in the mailbox," said Amy. "But, anyway, Maisie should have known whom I meant."

"It wasn't Maisie who gave me the letter," said Cassandra. "She's on vacation, and someone new is delivering the mail."

"That explains it," said Amy.

"We thought you were Cassandra the pig, and had come without a costume!" cried the goat.

"Wait," said Amy, "I'm declaring a special prize for our new friend, Cassandra the cat—Most Believable Costume *Ever!*" She took the gold star off her angel costume and handed it to Cassandra.

"I'm really glad you came," she said.

All the party guests cheered loudly—even Cassandra
the pig, who was happily polishing the silver star
Amy had given her for Most Royal Costume.

"Now let's have some more music," said Amy. "I'll
bring in the food."

The goat sat down at the piano and began to play again. The dog began to sing. Cassandra the pig adjusted her crown and began to clap in time to the music. The chicken and the cow began to dance. Then they beckoned to Cassandra to join them. She pulled off the rest of her pig costume, fluffed out her fur, and began to twirl around and around in the middle of all her new friends.